Madison
and the
Two Wheeler

Teach Your Children Well

By Dr. Vanita Braver
Illustrated by Carl DiRocco

STAR BRIGHT BOOKS
Cambridge Massachusetts

Published in the US by Star Bright Books, Inc.
The name Star Bright Books and the Star Bright Books logo
are registered trademarks of Star Bright Books, Inc.

Please visit: www.starbrightbooks.com. For orders,
email: orders@starbrightbooks.com, or call: (617) 354-1300.

Hardback ISBN: 978-1-59572-109-9
Star Bright Books / NY
Printed in China / WKT / 9 8 7 6 5 4 3 2

Paperback ISBN: 978-1-59572-688-9
Star Bright Books / MA / 00401220
Printed in China / WKT / 9 8 7 6 5 4

Printed on paper from sustainable forests.

Library of Congress Cataloging-in-Publication Data

Braver, Vanita.
 Madison and the two wheeler / by Vanita Braver ; illustrated by Carl DiRocco.
    p. cm -- (Teach your children well)
 Summary: When Madison tries to ride her bike without training wheels, she feels discouraged
at how hard it is, but with determination and the help of her parents, she finally succeeds.
  ISBN-13: 978-1-59572-688-9
 [1. Bicycles and bicycling --Fiction, 2. Determination (Personality trait) -- Fiction.]
 I. DiRocco, Carl, 1963- ill. II. Title.
 PZ7.B73795Mad2007
 [E]--dc22
                                          2006036048

To my loving husband Joel, with love.
Thank you for your encouragement, wisdom,
faith, humor, and loving kindness. —VB

To my parents. —CD

Madison was visiting her friend Emily. Some birds had made a nest near Emily's window.

"They are so cute," whispered Madison. "Look how big they are now!" The baby birds stretched their tiny wings.

"My mom says they are almost ready to learn to fly," Emily answered.

"I can ride my bike without training wheels, and it feels like flying!" said Emily.

"Hope can fly!" replied Madison, as she tossed her toy bluebird to Emily.

"Dad, will you help me learn to ride my bike without training wheels?" Madison asked that afternoon.

"Sure," said her dad, "we can do that now."

Soon the training wheels were off Madison's bike. As Madison helped her dad turn the bike right side up, it wobbled.

Madison's dad held the bike while she got on.

"Hold on and pedal," he said. "I am right here, keeping you steady."

Madison began to pedal. The front wheel wobbled. Riding without training wheels was harder than it looked. Then Madison felt the bike tipping over! Her dad caught the bike.

"Oops!" he said. "It's O.K., try again."

But Madison didn't feel so brave anymore.

"It's too scary, Dad. What if I fall?"
Madison asked.

"It takes time to get the hang of it,"
he answered. "Look ahead, not down at
the wheel. Aim for the mailbox."

The mailbox seemed very far away.
Madison put her feet back on the pedals
and started again. The handlebars wobbled.
The bike began to tip.

"Dad, stop!" shouted Madison.
"I don't want to ride anymore." She
jumped off the bike and ran into the house.

Her mom was in the living room.

"Mommy, I'll never learn to ride a two-wheeler. It's hopeless," said Madison.

"Honey, don't give up," Madison's mom soothed. "It takes time and hard work to learn anything new."

"But Mom," whined Madison, "I tried and tried, but I just can't balance! I'll never be able to do it."

"Madison, you have to believe you can do anything you set your mind to," her mom said. She picked up Hope, Madison's toy bluebird, and handed her to Madison. "And you have to practice over and over again. Do you want me to help?"

"No, thanks," Madison said, "I'm going to read." And she went and got a book.

"Madison, do you want to try your bike again?"
asked her dad the next morning.
"No, thanks," she replied.

Just then the phone rang. It was Emily.

"Guess what, Madison," she said. "The babies are learning
to fly! One of them can really fly now. My mom said you can
come over if you want. We can ride our bikes. Ask your mom!"

"Thanks, Emily," said Madison. "But not today."

As she hung up the phone, Madison thought about the baby birds. It must be so scary to jump off the edge of the nest for the very first time.

"Is riding a two-wheeler really like flying?" she wondered.

Then Madison saw Hope the Bluebird looking right at her. She picked her up and hugged her, and they went outside.

Madison put Hope in her bike basket. Her dad held the bike steady while Madison climbed on. Her mom held the handlebars.

"Come on, Honey, you can do it!" said her dad.

Madison began to pedal.

She rode a little way and almost lost her balance, but her mom caught her.

"That was great. Just keep trying," she said. "Look ahead to where you want to go."

Madison looked at the mailbox and pedaled. The bike wobbled, but she kept going. She was doing it! Just then the bike tipped! Madison tumbled onto the grass! She almost started to cry.

"Are you O.K?" called her dad.
Madison thought for a
moment and replied, "Sure."
Then she got back on her bike.

Again and again, Madison climbed back on her bike.
Each time the bike wobbled less, and she got better and better.
Finally, she shouted to her parents, "I can do it! Let go!"
Then she shouted, "Look!" and rode all the way to the mailbox.

Every day after school Madison practiced. And every day balancing on her bike became easier. On Friday, she rode to Emily's house. Emily was outside riding her bike.

"Your training wheels are gone!" said Emily. "That's great!"

"I can ride without them now," said Madison, "and it is like flying!"

That night, Madison's dad said, "It's great that you believed in yourself and did not give up. You and Emily will have lots of fun riding your bikes!" Then he tucked her in and kissed her good night.

"Good night, Daddy," said Madison, and she gave her dad a good night kiss right back.

Madison closed her eyes and then slowly opened them again. She smiled when she saw Hope the Bluebird.

Madison cuddled with Hope. Hope whispered into
Madison's ear, "Never give up! You should feel proud
because you worked hard and believed in yourself."
And with that, Madison fell asleep.

Parent's Note

Dear Parent or Educator,

As a mom of three, an educator, and a practicing child and adolescent psychiatrist, I know that parenting is challenging at best: I have often said that I was the perfect parent until I had children!

I want what we all want for our children—to have them lead happy, enriching, and successful lives. But no matter who we are, the essence of being human is to undergo a wide range of experiences, both good and bad. Life presents us all with moral dilemmas, discrepancies of the heart and mind. How we live our lives and cope with difficult circumstances is a reflection of who we are and the choices we make.

One of life's greatest gifts is the ability to reflect, to ask questions of each other and of ourselves. Through this process, we learn to make good choices—and it's a gift that must be nurtured and learned. The *Teach Your Children Well* series models the dialogue and interactions that facilitate the critical thinking and self-reflection necessary for kids to learn to make moral, ethical choices.

We can make a difference in the world through the way we, as individuals, conduct our lives. Our children are really our greatest resource!

Warmly,
Dr. Vanita Braver

Ten Tips for Raising Moral Children:

1. Make raising moral children a priority. If you really want to raise moral children, then commit to it and put forth the effort.
2. Live by setting a moral example. Research has shown that parents are the most significant and powerful influence in their children's moral development.
3. Be clear about what you value, and communicate that. You can't adequately instill a belief in your children if it's not clear within you.
4. Set clear, reasonable, and challenging guidelines about what you expect from your children. Reinforce these at every opportunity, but be open to discussion.
5. Set clear boundaries and enforce limits. Understand that all children will test limits, and be consistent in your responses.
6. Recognize opportunities to teach. The most powerful and persuasive moral teaching opportunities present themselves in ordinary moments.
7. Emphasize the Golden Rule. Encourage your children to treat others the way they wish to be treated.
8. Reflection is a powerful, effective tool to stimulate internal motivation. Encourage your children to think through the consequences of their actions and their effects on others.
9. Reinforce positive behaviors. When your children make good choices, notice their behavior and express to them how it made you feel.
10. Listen actively and allow your children to think through dilemmas. Ask them questions that allow them to draw conclusions.